No Roses for

by Gene Zion

HARRY!

Pictures by Margaret Bloy Graham

SCHOLASTIC INC.

New York Toronto London Auckland Sydney

ISBN 0-590-02393-4

Text Copyright © 1958 by Eugene Zion. Pictures © 1958 by Margaret Bloy Graham. This edition is published by Scholastic Inc., 730 Broadway, New York, NY 10003, by arrangement with Harper & Row, Publishers, Inc.

27 26 25 24 23 22 21 20 19   7 8 9/8
                                                              09

Printed in the U.S.A.

Harry was a white dog with black spots.
On his birthday, he got a present from Grandma.
It was a wool sweater with roses on it.
Harry didn't like it the moment he saw it.
He didn't like the roses.

When he tried it on, he felt cosy and snug.
But he still didn't like the roses.
He thought it was the silliest sweater
he'd ever seen.

The next day when Harry went into town
with the children, he wore his new sweater.
When people saw it, they laughed.
When dogs saw it, they barked.
Harry made up his mind then and there
to lose Grandma's present.

When they went into a big store to shop,
the children took off his sweater and let him
carry it. This was just what Harry wanted.

First he tried to lose it in the pet department—

but a man found it and gave it back.

Then he tried to lose it in the grocery department—

but a lady found it and gave it back.

He tried to lose it in the flower department—

but a little boy found it and gave it back.

The children didn't let Harry carry it any more.
They made him wear it. As they started home,
Harry was beginning to think he'd never lose it.

When he got home, his friends were waiting
to play with him. But Harry didn't feel like
playing, so they left him alone.

As he sat wondering what to do,
Harry noticed a loose stitch in his sweater.
He pulled at the wool — just a little at first —
then a bit more — and a little bit more.
Harry didn't know it, but a bird was watching.

In a minute, Harry had pulled out
quite a long piece of the wool.
The end of it lay on the grass behind him.
Suddenly the bird flew down.

Quick as a flash, she took the end of the wool
in her beak and flew away with it!
It all happened before Harry could even blink.

The sweater began to disappear right before
Harry's eyes. First one leg — then the neck —

then the other leg — then the back — and finally

the whole thing was just one long, long piece of
wool flying off into the sky. The sweater was gone!
Harry could hardly believe it.

He barked and jumped with joy!
Then he ran out of the yard.

He ran down the street barking thank you
to the bird over and over again.

The bird and wool were just a tiny speck in
the sky, but Harry kept following them.

He came home thirsty and tired, and was having
a drink in the kitchen when the children ran in.
"We got a letter from Grandma!" one of them said.
"She's coming to visit us!" shouted the other.
Harry thought of the sweater, and his tail drooped.

Before Grandma came, the family looked everywhere
for the sweater. They wanted her to see how nice
Harry looked in it. Of course they couldn't find it.
Only Harry knew why.

When Grandma arrived, Harry ran to her with
his leash. Then he sat up and begged.
"All right, Harry," said Grandma. "After I've had
my lunch and a nap, we'll go for a walk."

That afternoon, Harry and Grandma and the children
started off on their walk. Harry barked happily
and pulled toward the park.

When they got to the park, Harry pulled harder.
The children let him off his leash, and he ran on
ahead. He seemed to be looking for something.

All at once he stopped under a big tree.
He looked up and began to bark and wag his tail.
Grandma and the children came running.

They got to the tree and looked up too.
Suddenly one of the children said, "I see a **nest**!"
"It's made of **wool**!" said the other,
"and it has roses just like —"

"**Harry's sweater!**" they shouted together.

"It **is** Harry's sweater!" exclaimed Grandma.

Just then a bird looked out of the nest.

"Look! Grandma, look!" shouted the children.

"Harry gave his sweater to a bird!"

"I wonder how he did that!" said Grandma.

The bird sang, and Harry wagged his tail even harder.

At Christmas, Harry got a present from Grandma.
It was a **new** sweater!
Harry liked this one very much.
When he tried it on, he felt as cosy and snug
as the bird in the nest.
But best of all—it was white with black spots!